The White Lace Gloves

GILL VICKERY
Illustrated by ALEKSEI BITSKOFF

BLOOMSBURY

LONDON OXFORD NEW YORK NEW DELHI SYDNEY

FRANKLIN'S EMPORIUM

·EMPORIUM·

The White Lace Gloves

First published in 2016 by
Bloomsbury Education, an imprint of Bloomsbury Publishing Plc
50 Bedford Square, London, WC1B 3DP

www.bloomsbury.com

Bloomsbury is a registered trademark of
Bloomsbury Publishing Plc

ISBN 978 1 4729 1803 1

Typeset by Newgen Knowledge Works (P) Ltd., Chennai, India

Printed and bound by CPI Group (UK) Ltd, Croydon CR0 4YY

1 3 5 7 9 10 8 6 4 2

CONTENTS

THE BIRTHDAY PRESENT

I watched my cousin, Maisie, open the first of her birthday presents. I was as surprised as all the other guests when she screamed, threw the gift on the floor and jumped on it.

'Whatever's the matter?' Aunt Minty stooped down and picked the present up.

It was pair of white lace gloves with a designer label so famous even I recognised it.

'No!' Maisie pushed her mum's hand away. 'Get rid of them, they're horrible.'

'Just try them on, Maisie,' my Uncle Adrian snapped. You could tell he was embarrassed. His boss had bought the gloves and she wasn't looking too pleased.

Maisie burst into tears and ran off.

Everyone was mystified except me. As soon as I saw the gloves I knew what was wrong.

Chapter One
GOLDEN BAY

When Mum and Dad told me I was going to stay at the seaside with Dad's distant relatives, Adrian and Araminta, for practically the whole summer I didn't bother trying to make them change their minds. They never do.

Dad had lost his job and got a big redundancy payment. They'd decided to splash out and use some of it to go on a second honeymoon in Thailand. They wanted to experience the magic of the East. If it was magic they were after they should've gone to Golden Bay and let me go to Thailand.

Although I'd never been to Golden Bay before I checked it out and discovered it was weird, like a place from the olden days when kids rode donkeys and built sandcastles with tin buckets.

Things got weirder still when Mum and I caught the train to Golden Bay. Instead of going to the main train station we went to one a few miles out of town. It was like a film set for *The Railway Children*.

'What is this place?' I asked Mum.

'It's a Preserved Steam Trust.'

I was still mystified.

'When this line was closed ages ago, enthusiasts were allowed to buy it and run it. They keep up the old railway station and rescue steam engines as well.'

'I'd rather go by car.'

'Oh Alex, you know Dad had to drive to London and get the boys.'

My twin brothers, Ben and Sam, had finished university and Dad had gone to fetch them. They were artists and were coming home to set up their first big installation in a local gallery. That's why I couldn't stay with them while Mum and Dad were in Thailand: they said I'd get in the way.

'Anyway,' Mum went on, 'I'd have thought this was exactly the sort of place you like.'

She was right, in a way. The part of me that loves fantasy did like the Victorian ironwork, the old signs and the burping engines. It was very

steam punk. I started making up a story set at night in a deserted Victorian railway station. I was well into it and hardly noticed when we got a carriage all to ourselves and Mum stowed the cases on a netting rack above our heads. It didn't even register when we chuffed out of the station and down the track.

I was busy plotting a chase between a vampire and a woman private detective when Mum broke my concentration.

'That's a nuisance!'

The night-time cobbled streets and pounding feet faded from my mind. 'What is?' I asked.

Mum shook her phone. 'The signal keeps coming and going. Minty warned me that the connection was unreliable.'

Mum put the phone away and started reminiscing. I'd heard the stories before: how Mum had met Dad at university when he was sharing a house with Adrian, who'd just met Araminta. Mum went all wistful, like old people do when they go on about their student days, and I zoned out until I heard Mum say 'Maisie'.

Maisie was Araminta and Adrian's daughter. When my family went to stay with hers in London, which is where they live most of the year, Maisie

and I were expected to get along because there's only a couple of years between us. We didn't get on – at all. The adults never noticed.

'What about Maisie?' I asked cautiously.

Mum smiled at me. 'You'll have a lovely time together.'

Doing what? I thought. Building sandcastles and riding donkeys?

The engine gave a strangled whistle and heaved the train into another Victorian-looking station. A sign on the platform said, 'Golden Bay'.

Mum got the cases off the rack. I hitched up my bag and followed her onto the platform. 'There they are,' Mum said, and rushed up to Adrian, Araminta and Maisie. They did the usual hugging and kissing thing, then Mum nudged me forward. She was so excited she used the word she'd sworn not to: 'And here's my baby – hasn't she grown since you last saw her?'

I blushed a bright tomato red.

'Welcome, darling.' Araminta bent down and gave me a pecking sort of kiss on the cheek.

I glared at Mum through the cloud of expensive perfume hanging around Araminta like mist on a mountaintop. 'Don't call me that,' I hissed.

Mum giggled – which meant she was nervous – and said, 'Oh dear, Minty, she doesn't like to be

called that. It's a name the twins tease her with and she hates it.'

Too right I hate it. When Ben and Sam were younger and I was very little, they used to torment me with it if I tried to tag along with them and their friends. 'Go home, Baby,' they'd yell and all their friends would join in, chanting, 'Baby! Baby! Baby!'

It sent me into frothing rages. The boys and their friends only laughed louder and shouted, 'Baby!' all over again just to wind me up some more. The twins are OK now, more civilized and almost human compared with some lads, but I still hate being called 'Baby'.

'Never mind,' Adrian said in a smoothy way. 'Come and say hello to Maisie.'

Maisie stepped forward so that her back was to the grown-ups. 'Hi,' she said brightly, then mouthed, 'Baby'.

And that's how it all started. Every time we were on our own it was 'Baby' this and 'Baby' that. I ignored it as best I could though it was hard. She turned it on like a dripping tap – 'Baby, Baby, Baby,' drip, drip, drip – and it drove me CRAZY.

Chapter Two
DRESSES

Mum stayed with me for one night in Adrian and Minty's grand holiday home. It was a Regency house at one end of the sea front. She was well impressed with the bedroom we were given. It was pretty good – big with space for two double beds. It also had three windows.

'Triple aspect,' Mum said with a sigh. She watched those property programmes on TV and dual aspect was what she drooled over. Triple aspect was beyond wonderful.

She was also impressed with the en-suite bathroom. So was I, at first. No more fighting for the bathroom with two brothers, no more of their gruesome boxers left on the floor.

'Why's it got two doors?' I shook the handle of the one on the far wall. It was locked from the other side.

'It's a Jack-and-Jill bathroom,' Mum said. 'There must be another bedroom on the other side. They share the en-suite.'

I just knew that Maisie had the other room. The potions and lotions were all teen stuff with names like Wishes and Sizzle. The bathroom smelt like one of those cosmetics counters in a big store where they squirt perfumes at you as you walk by.

A gong sounded. 'Dinner,' Mum said.

They had a gong? Why didn't they yell up the stairs like normal people?

Dinner was good. Minty was a fantastic cook. It was about the only thing I did like once Mum had gone home.

There was one other thing I really enjoyed: Maisie and I were allowed to go off on our own in Golden Bay. We didn't often stay together though we were supposed to. Maisie usually met up with her friends and they hung about in a group on the pier. That was fine by me.

I explored the old town – narrow, cobbled streets, winding lanes, pastel painted houses; the promenade – rickety old pier, sea wall, little cove with fishing boats; the beach – sand, rock pools, donkeys and deckchairs; the cliffs – fabulous caves

at the base, a posh boarding school perched on the top; and, best of all, Franklin's Emporium.

Franklin's was a huge art deco department store, built about eighty years ago when Golden Bay was what my mum called, 'a playground for the wealthy'. Then the town went out of fashion and Franklin's closed down. It was put up for sale and let it out in 'units'.

I loved it from the first time I saw its seven storeys of peeling blue and white paintwork. Inside it was even better. It had marble floors and alabaster columns and a Ladies Room, all gilded like something out of the Arabian Nights. You could shoot a brilliant fantasy film in there.

When I wasn't exploring or reading fantasy novels I was at Franklin's. I could've almost enjoyed staying in Golden Bay if it hadn't been for Maisie's birthday and the white lace gloves.

Maisie and her friends had been birthday shopping solidly for a week and she'd tried on millions of dresses. It was great; it meant she was too busy to bother with me. That changed on the morning of the party.

I was lying on my bed reading when she burst into my bedroom through the connecting

bathroom. She had a green dress in one hand and a black one in the other.

'All right, Alex, which one?' she demanded, even though she didn't care what I thought. She only wanted to stop me reading because she knows I like it. Also, she wanted to show off. Those dresses must've cost a packet and she'd bought them from her massive clothes allowance which was more in a month than my total pocket money for a whole year.

I forced myself to look fascinated.

'The green one's nice. Try it on.'

That was a mistake. She tried the black one on, then the green one. Then the black one again with red shoes. Then the green one with toning sandals. Then the black one with gold sandals. It really did my head in. I could feel the words, 'This is dead boring,' writing themselves across my face.

Maisie read my expression. 'You might try and show some interest, BABY Alex. These are designer clothes,' she sneered.

It's interesting that sneer. It changes her face. It goes from being really, really pretty to all warped and lopsided like a wax head that's softened sideways in the sun.

I was fed up with Maisie. I got off the bed. 'Please yourself what you wear. You will anyway.'

Maisie flicked her long blonde hair over her shoulder. She did it gracefully, like one of those models in shampoo adverts, only it reminded me of a cat lashing its tail while it's making its mind up whether to savage you or not. I made a quick escape downstairs to the marquee that Minty and Adrian were busy organising for the party.

Minty was putting a glass vase full of pebbles supporting leafless, squiggly twigs onto a dazzling white tablecloth. I had to admire the time and effort she was putting in. At home we get paper tablecloths for parties, and paper serviettes. Minty calls them 'napkins' – she winces when I say serviettes, as if she's trodden on a nail.

'Can I help, Aunt Minty?' I offered, desperate to get away from Maisie.

I was too late. Maisie flounced through the tent flaps with a dress in each hand.

'Mummy, which of these looks best?'

Minty concentrated on sliding the vase about two centimetres to the right. 'They're both lovely, darling,' she said without even bothering to glance at Maisie.

Maisie pouted. 'You just don't care, do you?'

She had a point. One minute Minty and Adrian were drowning her in praise and adoration and the next they were so involved in their own things it was like Maisie was invisible. This was one of those times.

Adrian came in from the garden looking bulkier than usual. He'd got metres and metres of outdoor fairy lights slung round his middle.

'Daddy!' Maisie flounced forward and thrust the dresses under his nose. 'Mummy's no use to me at all. What do you think? Green or black?'

Adrian tried to struggle out of the flex like a fly trying to escape spider wrappings. 'I've got to get these strung up and then start on the rest of the lighting. Have to sort out those flares.'

Maisie's round blue eyes bulged in fury. There was going to be a row. I went back upstairs.

It was a big mistake. I should've gone to the Vermin Shed, which was where I did most of my reading. Adrian had christened it the Vermin Shed because it had loads of creepy crawlies in it: massive wolf spiders, woodlice, and even mice. That meant it had one big attraction for me; Maisie wouldn't go near it. When she realised that's where I kept disappearing to she did her waxy sneer and said, 'Vermin in the Vermin Shed. How appropriate.'

It didn't bother me. I loved that shed.

I was pretty sure Adrian was going to be in and out of it for the rest of the day, looking for things to make his outdoor lighting work. That was why I decided to go to my room instead.

I lay back on my bed, picked up *The Curse of the Hunter's Moon*, and started reading. The book was all about ravening werewolves and was a lot less scary than Maisie's tantrums. I got to read for a whole fifteen minutes before she came back. I was on chapter five when she appeared in the doorway.

'Green,' she said.

I turned over a page.

She came up to my bed and hovered there like a vulture. I knew I was doomed. I felt it in my bones.

'I need a pair of gloves to go with this dress,' she said.

I still didn't look up. 'In the middle of summer?'

'Don't pretend to be stupid, BABY.' She took a step nearer.

'Like I said, BABY Alex, I need a pair of gloves to go with this dress. I know it's hard for you to appreciate but I'm talking fashion here.'

I concentrated on my book. 'So?'

'So, I need time to get ready. So, you can go and get my gloves.'

I turned a page. 'Why should I?'

I felt the bed give as Maisie sat on the end. 'I know you don't want to come to my party and that's OK because I don't want you there either but Mummy would be mortified. She's told all her friends about how she's taken you in to help your parents out and they're expecting to see you. Get my gloves and I'll back you up if you tell her you feel sick and have to stay in bed tonight.'

I didn't trust Maisie to keep her side of the bargain, and I didn't like lying to Minty, but I didn't fancy being exhibited like a pet monkey either. I lowered my book.

'Give me some money then.'

Maisie did her horrible smirk and handed me thirty pounds in notes.

'What are these gloves like?' I asked her.

'White lace.' She stretched out a hand like she was trying on a glove for size, 'fingerless and with a little frill round the wrist.'

'Where am I supposed to find something like that?'

Maisie snatched *The Curse of the Hunter's Moon* off me. 'Try Franklin's.'

I cheered up immediately though I didn't let her see.

'Which unit?'

'I think there's some haberdashery unit that does scarves and things – they'll do gloves as well.'

'I don't suppose you know which floor?' I didn't fancy trawling all seven.

'No. You'll find it if you really want to miss my party.'

'Fine,' I said.

Maisie snapped my book shut and tossed it on my bed. 'Baby trash,' she said.

'Trash yourself,' I said and I ran all the way to Franklin's to burn off my temper.

Chapter Three
FRANKLIN'S EMPORIUM

Although Golden Bay is old-fashioned it's still popular, especially with families, and when I pushed through the front door at Franklin's I saw that it was packed with grockles. That's what Maisie and her friends call them. I call them tourists and Mum calls them holidaymakers. Maisie thinks they're common but they've paid their money and they're entitled to be there just as much as she is. And I'm a grockle too, in a way, except I wouldn't have come within fifty miles of Maisie and her parents if I'd had a choice whereas real grockles save up all year for the chance to go to Golden Bay.

My trainers squeaked across the marble floor as I wove through the people wandering around the big, glamorous entrance hall and made my way to the notice board by the lift.

The board was crammed with cards pinned in different sections according to what floor the unit was on. *Dragon's Bane Fighting Fantasy* was on the second floor, *Black Cat Bookshop* on the third, *Caruso's Gelateria* on the fourth and so on. *Papertape*, the stationer's, had CLOSED written across it in red. A lot of the units were there and gone quicker than a hungry grockle's bag of chips. I'll miss *Papertape*, I thought, scanning the board for a card saying 'haberdashery'. There wasn't one.

That was when I made my next big mistake. If I had a problem or I needed to remember something I made up rhymes. When I did it at school it drove the teachers mad, especially Mr Polemounter, our history teacher, who was ancient and liked a lot of quiet in his lessons. Once, when we were doing the 17th century witch persecutions, I wanted to remember 1612, the date of the Pendle trials, and I started muttering:

'One, six, one, two
Was when the witches made their brew.'

Mr Polemounter had peered down his long nose and told me to be careful or I might find

myself casting a spell by accident. I thought he was being sarcastic and took no notice. Anyway, I didn't believe in magic, not then.

As I stood in front of the notice board I found myself muttering:

'I need a haberdashery
To buy some gloves of white.
I'm in a fix – slash – hurry,
Please bring the shop to light.'

'Scuse me!' A family rushed past me to the lift. They were looking at me a bit strangely. There was a skinny little mum and a very big suede-head dad in a tight T-shirt with a rude motto on it. There were also four children, yelling and scrapping. The draught the family made as they swirled past fluttered a fallen card along the floor like a confused moth. I picked it up.

Harriette's Haberdashery, it read in old-fashioned letters. Underneath in small lettering was:

Come and see our unrivalled collection of ribbons and bows, feathers, sequins and shells; belts, caps, scarves and shawls and a hundred other small delights gathered from all over the world.

Though it didn't mention gloves, it was start. It didn't mention which floor the haberdashery was on either but I could always ask the liftman, he'd know. It was his job.

The liftman was another strange thing about Franklin's Emporium. It was as though he'd been left over from the days when Franklin's was a thriving store. Apart from being very old he was like those liftmen you see in black and white films. He had a uniform, blue with a crest of three gold crowns on the pocket. And he had epaulettes, with gold edging, on his shoulders.

I pressed the call button and waited. The lift pinged and the outer doors opened to show a sort of black, concertina grille. The liftman pulled the grille to one side and I got into the lift.

'D'you know where Harriette's Haberdashery is?' I asked, waving the card at him.

He pressed a button to make the doors shut and closed the grille.

'I heard you summon Harriette,' he said in a dry papery voice. 'What do you want of her?'

That wasn't what I'd expected. I'd been in the lift loads of times before and never heard the liftman say anything much except to ask which floor or say, 'Mind the doors please'. Besides, I

didn't understand. How could he have heard me say anything? He'd been working in his lift.

I should've known something strange was going on, what with all the fantasy I've read but I was in a hurry and I didn't believe in magic.

'I only want a pair of gloves.' I held up my watch. 'And I haven't got much time.'

His old eyes were very bright under massive eyebrows sprouting in all directions. 'Why do you wish for gloves?'

I was going to be stuck talking to him for hours at this rate. I sighed.

'They're not for me. They're for my sort-of cousin and she wants them now, or more like yesterday, because she's a spoilt brat and she'll make my life a misery if I don't come up with them soon.'

The call sign flashed red and hands hammered on the door.

'Hadn't you better let them in?' I said.

'Let them wait.' Shadows seemed to cluster round the old liftman in his corner, patient as a spider. His eyes glittered.

'Tell me about your cousin.'

Although it was none of his business I knew I had to go along with him if I was going to get out of that lift. It wasn't that I thought he was evil or dangerous but he was definitely a bit weird. I decided to try and make him feel sorry for me.

'Oh she's horrible. She orders me around like I'm her personal servant and she makes fun of me. She calls me BABY all the time even though she knows I hate it – especially because she knows I hate it.'

Until that moment I hadn't realised how much Maisie had got to me. I was filled with towering rage that took me by surprise. Without meaning to I found myself accidentally making a rhyme: 'It's time that the baby was her – I'd love it if only she were.'

The lift dropped. It happened so quickly I had to grab the handrail running round the side and I banged my elbow. It hurt.

We jerked to a stop and the old man pulled back the black grille.

'Basement,' he said in his papery voice as the doors slid open.

'Thanks.' I rushed out, glad to be away from the freaky liftman.

The dark, musty basement was completely different from the rest of the store. For a start there were no people and for another thing it was crammed full of unwanted stuff left over

from the days when Franklin's was a busy department store: ancient counters and display stands; the shrivelled skeletons of dead plants in massive cracked pots; three-legged chairs and splintered tables. And, right down the middle, mannequins with painted, old-fashioned faces leaned against each other in two crooked rows leaving a narrow alleyway between them. Everything was dusty and tied up in cobwebs. Normally I'd have loved it, but not then. I turned back to the liftman.

'This isn't the right place – it's all empty down here.'

He nodded towards the end of the basement, shrouded in darkness. 'Harriette is waiting for you.'

The doors closed and the lift whirred upwards before I had enough sense to press the call button and stop it from moving.

'Silly old fool,' I grumbled. Now I'd have to find the stairs, climb up and check out all the floors till I found where *Harriette's* really was.

A faint light I hadn't noticed before glimmered at the end of the basement. Maybe it was an illuminated sign over the stairs. I had to go down the alleyway of lurching pink mannequins to reach it.

At first it wasn't too bad even though they were creepy, what with them being partly dressed and missing the odd limb or head, but halfway along they were packed closer together. They pressed in on me. I knocked an arm I hadn't noticed sticking out. It flopped down and hung out of its socket as if it was dislocated. I tried to slot it back and it came away in my hands.

'Sorry,' I said.

Why was I apologising to a shop dummy, especially one in a flesh-pink corset fastened up with hooks and eyes? I glared at it. Its painted lips simpered and one eye dropped shut in a knowing wink.

My heart jumped and so did I – straight into a bald mannequin with a swirly painted moustache. It reeled into the other dummies. They toppled towards me like an army being mown down in slow motion.

I raced off. They picked up speed and came crashing towards me like huge, people-shaped dominoes. I shot round the corner at the end of the basement just as they crashed deafeningly to the floor. About a hundred years' worth of dust billowed round the corner and almost choked me.

I leaned against the wall while the dust settled and I got my breath back. Maisie owes me big time for this, I thought savagely. 'Next time you can get your own stupid gloves,' I wheezed.

A rumbling noise made me turn. A wooden head rolled round the corner and stopped with its blue glass eyes fixed on me. It gave me the creeps. I looked the other way. And there it was, in front of me, *Harriette's Haberdashery*, all alone in the darkness.

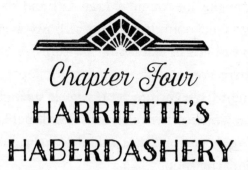

Chapter Four
HARRIETTE'S HABERDASHERY

Harriette's Haberdashery stood in the spotlight of a hanging lantern. It was tiny, not much bigger than a tall wardrobe but beautiful, so beautiful.

It was shaped like a tent and the material was a deep silky blue scattered all over with golden stars. Inside it was mad with colour: scarlet ribbons and emerald scarves looped about like Christmas garlands, glass beads and pearl buttons glittered from jars, huge soft feathers of aquamarine and emperor's purple swayed in pots, and cushions and rugs were heaped all over the floor. I sucked in a deep breath of amazement and my nostrils filled up with a scent I couldn't place.

'Can I help you?' a small child's voice said.

I hadn't noticed the little girl till then and I jumped in surprise. She laughed. Nobody likes being made fun of by a little kid and so when I answered I sounded almost as bossy as Maisie. 'Who's in charge here?'

'There's only me.'

'Right.' This had to be Harriette's daughter or sister or some other relative, I decided. Harriette must've gone for a break and left the little girl minding the shop.

Her eyes were so dark they looked black, like a raven's, and her silky dark hair, all beaded and braided with silk threads, was as glossy as feathers. She was like an old-fashioned hippy, what with the beads and her long cinnamon coloured dress sewn all over with tiny pieces of mirror.

'What sort of gloves would you like?' she asked.

'Pardon?' The colours and scents were making me feel a bit peculiar and I didn't remember telling her I wanted gloves.

The little girl chuckled. For some reason I thought of wood smoke on the wind.

'Silk or satin?' she asked. 'Cotton or woollen? Sateen or suede? Velvet, velveteen or lace?'

'Lace – white lace.'

She burrowed under a mound of mossy green cushions like a squirrel foraging for hazel nuts, and pulled out a cedar wood box carved with rosebuds. She opened it. 'Choose.'

I picked out a pair of gloves, fingerless, like Maisie wanted, with a frill of flowers round the wrist. 'How much?'

'Five pounds.'

It didn't seem a lot. 'Are you sure?' I didn't want her to get into trouble with whoever owned the unit.

'Quite sure, thank you.'

She took the money and put the gloves in a paper bag. It was printed in blue and white stripes and on it was a logo of three golden crowns.

She pointed. 'The stairs are over there.'

'Thanks.'

I ran. My mind was full of Maisie otherwise I'd have thought, that's funny, I don't remember telling her I wanted the stairs. Instead, I thought, never, never will I come back to Golden Bay. Next holiday I'd better be taken to somewhere really good – like Transylvania – to make up for being Maisie's servant this summer.

I sprinted all the way back to the house and flew upstairs to Maisie's room. She was wearing

the green dress and strutting in front of her mirror as though she were on a catwalk.

'Well?'

I held up the paper bag.

Maisie did her warped-wax face; she was used to designer packaging.

'The gloves are OK,' I said, a bit defensively.

She tweaked the bag off me like it was infected with the Black Death and shook out the gloves. They fitted her perfectly. She crumpled up the bag and tossed it into her waste paper basket.

I waited for her to say something sarcastic and insist I go back and find a better pair. Instead she looked at them in a surprised, sleepy sort of way and said, 'Hm, very nice.'

She sat on the bed as if her legs had suddenly turned to jelly and slithered down against the pillows.

'I think I'll have a little nap,' she murmured and snuggled up to her pillow like a baby resting against its mum's shoulder. She dozed off – just like that – in her designer dress and the white lace gloves. She even kept her gold sandals on.

I was totally astonished. It wasn't only that she'd dropped off like Sleeping Beauty after she'd pricked her finger on the spindle – it was that she never, ever did anything to crumple her best

clothes, or any of her clothes. None of her family did. Even when Adrian mowed the lawn he wore designer casuals. The minute he'd finished the clothes went in the wash and he put new ones on. My dad's got gardening clothes that look like they came out of the ark and probably had their last wash when the Great Flood arrived.

I didn't know what to do. If I woke Maisie she might be in a bad temper, decide she didn't like the gloves after all and order me back to Franklin's to get a different pair. I'd had enough of running around for the morning. I decided to fetch my book and go to the Vermin Shed. I'd be safe from Maisie in there.

I left the house and ran through the sloping garden, past the maze and the pond that's the size of a small lake, through the copse and into the kitchen garden where the Vermin Shed was, in between the compost heap and the fire pit.

I pushed open the creaking door and went in. Although it was packed with loads of stuff – half-empty tins of paint, jars of nails and screws, curled up hoses and the gardening man's own tools – it was very tidy. The gardening man liked it that way.

I slumped in the old armchair squashed under the window and wriggled into a comfy position

with my back against one arm and legs over the other. The shed was as peaceful as an empty church. Sunlight shimmered through the window. A spider abseiled up and down an invisible thread and a woodlouse trundled across one arm of the chair.

I turned a page of *The Curse of the Hunter's Moon*. A werewolf howled its ancient agony at the cold Transylvanian moon.

The shed door burst open.

'Must find those flares,' Adrian said.

I shut my book and stood up.

'No need to move,' Adrian said.

I left anyway. I knew I'd never get any peace with Adrian shifting things and upsetting the gardener's tidy shed. I went back upstairs thinking I might manage to get some reading in if Maisie was still asleep. As I passed by her open door I heard a strange whiffling noise. I poked my head round the door to see what was causing it.

Maisie was still curled up on her bed, fast asleep, as I'd left her. But she had changed. Totally and utterly changed.

Chapter Five
BACK TO THE EMPORIUM

I went cold as I stared at her tiny little body, her bald head and her toothless, slobbery mouth. The only familiar thing about her was the waxy sneer that flickered across her dreaming face.

I stood, skewered to the spot, staring pop-eyed at the shrunken figure lying in the middle of the green dress like a frog in Adrian's pond, and tried to work out what had happened. Nothing could explain the transformation.

Then I remembered.

I remembered the little girl in her starry tent.

I remembered the old man in the lift.

I remembered I'd made a crazy wish.

And I remembered Mr Polemounter's warning.

I groaned. I should've listened to him. My habit of making up rhymes had got me into trouble, big time, exactly like he said it would. I'd made up a spell that summoned Harriette and then I'd made that stupid wish as well. I'd got exactly what I'd wished for; Maisie was a baby.

She stirred in her sleep, rolled over and drooled on the dress. There was only one thing to do. Praying Maisie wouldn't wake up, I wrapped the designer dress round her like a very expensive blanket, picked her up, sneaked out of the house and went back to Franklin's, fast. By the time I got there my arms were killing me. I was amazed that a thing as small as baby Maisie was that heavy. I lugged her across to the lift and pressed the call button.

'Ain't she cute!' a voice said.

Cute? I thought. Who'd be deranged enough to see Maisie as cute?

It was the family I'd seen earlier. They stood around me eating super-grande ice creams from *Caruso's Gelateria*. The suede-head dad chucked Maisie under the chin with one of his massive, sausage-like fingers.

She burped. The whole family laughed.

I felt a warm, damp sensation spreading down my front.

'Y'know, our Nikki, she's just like our Sarah was at that age,' the dad said to the mum.

'You're not wrong, Matt,' the mum said.

'She your sister?' one of the little kids asked me.

'No, she's. . .' The lift pinged. The doors opened. I stepped in. '. . . my sort-of-cousin,' I finished, glaring at the liftman.

He drew back the grille and I pressed the 'Close Doors' button with my good elbow. 'Change Maisie back,' I demanded.

He didn't pretend not to understand. 'You summoned Harriette with your spell, you asked a thing of her and you made a wish of me. You have what your heart desired.'

'I didn't mean it when I said I wished Maisie was a baby – not a real baby. It was only a way of speaking. Change her back.'

The old man stood in his corner, waiting. Maisie burped again and drooled some more. She yawned and stretched as if she was going to wake up.

'Please,' I said quickly to the old man. It came out sort of desperate, although I was trying to sound humble.

'You will have to make another request of Harriette and another wish of me.'

'Fine.'

I thought furiously. A rhyme came into my head:

'I'll ask from her a second pair
Of gloves all lacy, white and fair.'

The damp patch down my front was getting bigger.

I glowered at the old man and chanted:

'My wish of you is somewhat bolder –
Please make Maisie much, much older.'

I was caught off balance as the lift leapt upwards. I banged my other elbow.

The lift stopped, the old man drew back the grille and opened the doors.

'Top floor,' he said in his dry, old voice.

'Harriette's is in the basement,' I objected.

The liftman pointed a knobbly finger into a vast, deserted terrace restaurant with a bank of windows overlooking the bay. At the far end was Harriette's starry tower. I didn't have time to wonder how *Harriette's Haberdashery* had managed to move from top to bottom of the store in such a short space of time. I was too worried about

Minty and Adrian finding out that their daughter had turned into a baby and falling down dead with shock.

I muttered, 'Go for it,' to myself and ran to the silken tent through the maze of upturned chairs and tables – which wasn't easy with a fat baby in my arms.

Instead of a little girl, an old lady sat knitting just inside the tent. Despite her white hair and wrinkled skin there was a definite resemblance to the little girl. She had the same bird-bright dark eyes and when she spoke the same smoke-on-the-wind voice. She smiled.

'It's gloves you want, isn't it my dear?'

'Yes please, white lace ones.'

She got up in a swirl of cinnamon skirts, the little mirrors glinting like raindrops. She moved a pile of midnight blue cushions and reached for an ebony box dotted with pearly moons. She lifted the lid. 'Choose.'

I plunged my hand in and took the first pair I touched. 'How much?'

'Ten pounds.'

I paid and the old lady gave me the gloves in another blue and white stripy bag.

'Thank you.'

She smiled, nodded and went back to her knitting.

I wove my way back through the chairs and tables to the lift and pressed the call button. It didn't light up. I groaned. I was going to have to carry this lump down seven flights of stairs and walk all the way home.

I hitched Maisie up, leaned her over one shoulder and looked round the terrace. The old lady pointed with a knitting needle. Away in a corner was an open door with 'Stairs', painted above it. I groaned again and set off.

I was done for when I got back to the house and I was worried about what might happen if I bumped into Minty and Adrian. They'd be very surprised to see me carrying a baby, especially one that was a mini-Maisie. Luckily for me they were still in the marquee making party arrangements. I panted up the stairs and into Maisie's room without them seeing me.

I dumped Maisie on her bed. Now what? I thought. Nothing happened – she stayed a baby.

I thought harder. The first gloves had turned Maisie into a baby. Maybe I had to take them off.

It's hard getting gloves off a baby. They've got these really small, wriggly hands like demented

starfish. It's even harder trying not to wake them up while you're doing it.

Once I'd got the gloves off I didn't know what to do with them. Maisie wouldn't want them. I decided to put them in the paper bag and get rid of them as soon as I could.

I got the bag out of my pocket, took the new gloves out and put the first pair in. Just as I shoved the bag back into my jeans, Maisie opened her eyes wide. She took one look at me, screwed her face up and bawled.

'Shush!' I hissed at her.

She screamed even louder.

Think! I told myself desperately. What had made Maisie drop off to sleep before? Of course: putting the gloves on.

I jammed the new ones on her hands. A whole screwed-up little fist fitted into the palm part. Maisie stopped shrieking and hiccupped.

'Nice Maisie,' I said.

She glared. Her mouth quivered and opened to let out a scream. The glove magic began to work. She managed one evil look from under half-closed eyelids then sagged into the green dress like a deflated balloon and whiffled a small snore.

I sank onto the end of the bed in relief.

Maisie began to change. I watched in horrible fascination as she went from baby to toddler in seconds. It made me feel a bit queasy, especially the teeth suddenly bursting out of her gums.

As she grew older her fingers got caught up in the lace and I had to untangle them and poke them through the finger holes. It wasn't that creepy as the growing began to slow down once Maisie got to about six or seven.

I decided to leave. I definitely didn't want to be there when Maisie woke up. Not with the designer dress all crumpled and specky with drool. Not to mention the wet patches.

I quickly changed my soggy T-shirt and ran downstairs into the hallway. I cannoned straight into Adrian. He gave a snort, 'pfff,' and clutched his midriff.

'Sorry! Sorry!'

'Not your fault, Alex,' Adrian puffed.

He took a few deep breaths. 'We heard screaming coming from upstairs. I was on my way to investigate.'

He squinted at me suspiciously. 'What was going on? You and Maisie haven't come to blows have you?'

'Oh no, Uncle Adrian.' I laughed cheerfully.

Adrian narrowed his eyes even more suspiciously. I never laugh like that. I usually laugh sarcastically.

'Cats – it was tomcats fighting – they screamed like babies. Horrible.'

Minty appeared. 'Well, what was it?' she demanded. She sounded stressed. Maybe the party arrangements were getting to her.

'Tomcats, Araminta, brawling,' Adrian said.

'Really?' Minty wasn't stupid.

I backed towards the door. 'Yes, I saw them. That big black and white one from next door and a Siamese I haven't seen before. It was a chocolate point,' I added, describing my best friend's cat, hoping it made my story more believable.

'Siamese, that would explain it,' Adrian said. 'They can make one hell of a noise.'

I fled outside. The garden flares were stacked neatly by the marquee, which meant Adrian wouldn't need to go back to the Vermin Shed. That suited me fine. I needed a rest after everything that had happened.

I'd left my book behind but it didn't matter. I'd got a whole stack of others in the shed. I'd bought them from the *Black Cat Bookshop* at Franklin's. I chose one of my favourites, *The Mummy's*

Revenge, and settled back in the old armchair. I immediately got lost in the story and forgot all about Maisie and the gloves. I reached one of the best parts where the mummy is lurching through foggy London streets bemoaning its fate, tearing bandages from its ravaged visage with hands that are nothing but shrivelled claws, their nails curved into blackened talons. The last wrapping tears away and the mummy's hideous face, shrivelled and leathered, feels the first breath of air on its skin for thousands of years.

A tap at the window broke the spell.

I looked up. There, peering at me through the window, eyes burning with hatred, was the mummy.

Chapter Six
THE MUMMY'S REVENGE

The mummy's head wobbled at me from the top of a skinny neck, knobbly as a stick of Brussels sprouts. Its lipless mouth opened, its tongue flapped in its almost toothless mouth and it croaked, 'Help me.'

No chance. I was staying safe inside the Vermin Shed.

The thing disappeared. The door handle began to rattle.

I leapt out of the chair and turned the key in the lock. The door shook as the mummy pounded on it. 'Let me in!'

Never.

The mummy appeared at the window again. Its face was screwed up in fury and its withered fist hammered on the window till I thought the glass was going to break.

'Alex, come out and help me!'

It knew my name? I looked more closely at the wizened face pressed against the glass. Even though it looked like a squashed toad I recognized the scowl. The green dress flapping round the bony shoulders was familiar as well. And the lace gloves on its clenched hands.

The mummy-thing was Maisie.

A horrible thought crept into my mind. This was my fault. I'd got the second spell all wrong. I'd asked the liftman to make Maisie, 'much, much older,' and he had, literally.

'I didn't mean make her ancient,' I muttered guiltily as I unlocked the shed door.

The second I was outside, Maisie clamped a claw-like hand on my wrist and shook me, hard. She had a lot of strength for someone that old.

'You've got to help me, Alex.'

Long nails dug into my skin. The ancient eyes, like wrinkly raisins poked into a pudding, spilled tears. 'Mummy and Daddy threw me out. They didn't want to listen to me.'

I wasn't surprised; I didn't want to listen either but I couldn't help it. Mummified Maisie was horribly fascinating.

'You will help me, won't you, Alex. You're always reading about this sort of thing – you understand how it works. You can make me myself again.'

I didn't particularly want Maisie to be herself again, acting superior and trying to make my life a misery with her sneering and her taunting, but she didn't deserve what had happened to her. Of course I was going to help. Anyway, I felt guilty for fooling about with magic and making a mess of it.

Maisie began to wheedle. 'You're so clever, Alex. I know you can do it.'

She was pathetic.

We went to Franklin's. It took a while. Maisie's tottering, 3,000 year old legs were like sticks and I was worried they'd break if we went too fast or she tripped. I just hoped no one was going to stop me and ask what I was doing with bad–sight–of–the–week clinging to my arm like a living nightmare. To take my mind off it, I told Maisie the whole story of the liftman, the wishes and *Harriette's Haberdashery*.

She wasn't pleased. 'It's your fault. You've done this to me.'

I couldn't deny it. 'I didn't do it on purpose,' I said. 'I'll get it right this time.'

The claw squeezed tighter, like a manacle. 'You'd better.'

We reached Franklin's at last and Maisie followed me through the revolving doors into the lobby.

The grockle family were on their way out. I accidentally trod on one of the little kid's toes. He yelped and stuck his tongue out at me. Maisie peered over my shoulder at him. He howled in terror.

'Now wait a minute. . .' The dad picked the boy up and advanced towards Maisie. She hissed like a maddened snake and the whole family stepped back. The other children began to cry and Maisie hissed louder than ever.

'Stop it!' I dragged Maisie to the lift and banged on the lift button. The doors opened immediately and as soon as the old man pulled the grille to one side I shoved Maisie inside.

I didn't bother discussing the rules with the liftman. I knew them by now – only too well.

'I ask of Harriette a final pair,

Of white lace gloves for her...' I glared at Maisie, '...to wear.'

I turned my glare on the liftman. He was very, very still in his shadowy corner. According

to everything I've read in fantasy, there's a rule of three in magic. I'd asked Harriette for three pairs of gloves and now I was making a third wish from the liftman. It was my last chance to get Maisie back to normal. I thought flattery might help.

'My wish of you, O mighty mage,
Is, make this girl her rightful age,' I gabbled.

Nothing happened. My mind whirred. What else did he want – respect? That snarky thought made me feel a bit uneasy; the old man had tried to help me put my accidental spell-making right. I thought up another verse and spoke more humbly.

'I beg you through my flowing tears,
Restore her to her proper years.'

I wasn't actually crying but it was the best I could do on the spur of the moment. It worked. The lift jerked upwards to the third floor with its rows of units and browsing customers. The liftman pointed with his gnarly finger. Through the strolling groups of shoppers I saw the top of Harriette's blue pavilion.

We got out and I turned to thank the old man. Too late, the lift doors were closing and I only caught a glimpse of him. His hand was raised in farewell and his face looked sad. I waved back, though I don't think he saw me.

'Hurry up,' Maisie snarled.

I turned away from the lift, steered her towards the tent and parked her behind a bank of ostrich plumes to screen her from shoppers.

This time Harriette was a young woman and she was waiting for us. She held a sandalwood box, studded all over with brass suns. She opened it. There was only one pair of gloves inside.

Maisie started trying to tear off the gloves she was wearing. She couldn't manage it by herself and I had to do it for her. It wasn't pleasant; the leathery ridges and bony lumps on her hands kept getting snagged in the lace. And she was shaking.

I managed it at last and tried to stuff the gloves in my pocket. It was already full with the first pair of gloves I'd put in the bag and forgotten about. I put the second pair into the bag and squashed the whole lot back into my jeans.

'Hurry up!' Maisie snarled.

I worked the new gloves over her mummified hands.

Maisie held them up and stared, mesmerized.

'How much?' I asked Harriette.

'Fifteen pounds,' she said in her smoke-on-the-wind voice. I paid her the last of Maisie's money and she went behind a curtain at the back of the tent. We got out as fast as Maisie's ancient legs would let us. It was the last I ever saw of Harriette.

'C'mon.' I led Maisie to the stairs, tucked away in a corner. We had to go past a fancy dress unit which was a good thing as Maisie didn't look out of place next to the zombie outfits on display.

Halfway down the stairs Maisie began to change again. Her mahogany skin flaked off in strips like old wallpaper. Ancient brown stumps of teeth wobbled free and dropped with a 'plink, plink, plink' on the stone steps. I decided I didn't want to see any more and ran down the stairs. I waited at the bottom. Maisie's footsteps got nearer. They stopped. I turned, slowly, hoping to see Maisie back to her normal self.

She was.

Chapter Seven
TRAPPED

On the way home Maisie's mouth was sealed tighter than a super glued envelope. She stared straight ahead and marched on, head up, the grubby green dress flapping round her. People stared, and not in the way she was used to. They laughed. She took no notice. By the time we reached the house I couldn't help admiring her. She hadn't complained once.

We went in by the back door and up to her bedroom without Minty or Adrian catching us. I closed the door, leaned back on it and breathed a sigh of relief. Maisie pulled off the gloves, dropped them on the bed and went into the bathroom. I heard the key turn.

I knocked on the door. 'Let me know when you're done,' I said. I needed to get cleaned up

too. All that ancient, peeling skin had creeped me out and made me want a good scrub down. Besides which, there was still the party to get ready for.

Maisie didn't answer. All I heard was the shower going and the clink of beauty treatment bottles. She was going to be a long time. I decided I might as well go to my room and pick up where I'd left off with *The Curse of the Hunter's Moon*.

As I lay back on my bed I felt an uncomfortable lump under my bum. It was the paper bag with the first two pairs of gloves. I'd had enough of them. I took the bag out, screwed it up even tighter and lobbed it into the wastepaper basket.

Maisie barged into my room about an hour later. She was in a bathrobe, with her hair in a towel. One arm was stretched out in front of her and the third pair of gloves dangled between her finger and thumb.

'These gloves you got me are rubbish.' She dropped them on the floor, wiped her fingers on her bathrobe and held out her hand, palm up.

'Give me my money.'

I gawped in astonishment. I couldn't help it.

'I used it all,' I reminded her. 'There's no change.'

'For a pair of scabby gloves? I don't think so.' She clicked her fingers. 'My money, BABY Alex.'

I felt my temper building up. Maisie knew I hadn't meant for the magic to happen and I'd done my best to put it right.

'It was three pairs, remember?' I snapped.

'What are you talking about?'

'I had to pay for three pairs. Those,' I tipped my head at the gloves on the floor, 'and the ones that turned you into a baby and a shrivelled old hag.'

Maisie went pale. Then she flushed and did her waxy sneer. 'That ridiculous tale you came up with? It was just a stupid story like the ones you're forever reading.'

She was doing what she always did: persuading herself that what she didn't like didn't exist or hadn't happened. It wound me up when she was caught out getting me in trouble and then denying she was involved. She was convincing enough to pass a lie detector test. Adrian and Minty believed her every time. I was going to let it go, as usual, but then she went too far.

'Grow up, BABY Alex,' she said.

That was one 'baby' too many. I jumped up, ran to the wastepaper basket and fished out the paper bag.

'What about these then?' I shook the gloves onto the bed.

Maisie stared at them in horror. Her eyes bulged like gobstoppers and she recoiled until her back was pressed against the wall.

'Get rid of them!' she snarled.

Though I didn't particularly want to touch them, I picked the gloves up off the floor and managed to get all three pairs into the bag and folded the top over.

'Burn them!' Maisie ordered. 'Now.'

I didn't argue – burning the gloves was a good idea. I went straight to the fire pit in the kitchen garden. When I got there my heart sank; Adrian was standing in the doorway of the Vermin Shed.

'Ah, Alex, come and help me with the posthole diggers.' He disappeared into the shed.

What was he up to now? I followed him into the shed.

'Here you are.' Adrian ferreted out two digging tools and handed me one. 'Come on, I'll show you what to do. We're going to plant those flares. The gardener's cancelled; he's not well.' He rushed out of the shed.

I was sorry for the gardener but I was glad for me. Digging holes was better than getting ready

for the party, and it kept me away from Maisie. On the other hand, I wasn't going to get a chance to burn the gloves, at least not straightway. I grabbed a half-empty jar labelled 'nails – large', stuffed the paper bag inside and pushed it to the back of a shelf.

I was worried about leaving the bag there. Adrian was in and out of the shed all the time and might find it by accident. I'd have to get it back as soon as possible.

I ran out after Adrian and helped him with the flares. He asked my opinion on where to position them and took notice of what I said. That made a change from being ordered around by Maisie. We dug holes and planted the big flares round the pond and along the pathways and the smaller ones around the bottom of the maze hedge.

When we'd finished Adrian stood back and leaned on his spade, a pleased smile on his face. 'It's going to look good.' He gave me a hearty slap on the back. I staggered. He was too busy feeling proud of himself to notice and I was too happy being out of Maisie's way to care about being winded.

'Better go inside, get dolled up for the party and all that,' Adrian said. 'Time's getting on.'

When I got upstairs Maisie was waiting for me. 'Well, did you burn them?'

I hesitated.

She stepped forward. 'You didn't, did you?'

I shook my head. 'I didn't get the chance. I've put them in the shed. I'll get rid of them later.'

'You'd better,' Maisie said.

'Or what?'

Maisie took another step forward, eyes squinting with hate.

I needed an exit. I shot into the bathroom and slammed the door. I bolted it quickly as Maisie threw herself on it and hammered furiously. I rushed to the other door and bolted that too, just in time. Maisie began pounding on it with both fists.

'What's going on?' Minty's voice carried through Maisie's demented shrieks and the thundering on the door.

'Go away, Mummy!' Maisie shouted.

'I shall do as I please in my own house,' Minty said. She was very calm. I suppose she thought Maisie was having one of her usual meltdowns.

She tapped on the bathroom door. 'Alex dear, are you in there?'

I felt safe enough to come out.

'Now girls,' Minty said crisply, 'why are you fighting?'

'She doesn't want to come to my party,' Maisie said.

'It's not that...' I clutched my stomach and was about to make pathetic groaning noises when Maisie said, 'She was going to pretend she didn't feel well so she could stay in bed and read her precious books.'

'Is that true, dear?' Minty looked disappointed.

'Not exactly.' I didn't like lying. Apart from the fact that it was wrong, it wasn't Minty and Adrian's fault that Maisie had made my life miserable. I tried to sound reasonable. 'I'm not really into parties.'

Minty gave me an understanding look. 'I know this kind of grand party might seem daunting if you're not used to it but you'll love it if you give yourself a chance.'

I gave in. 'All right, I'll go.'

'That's settled then.' Minty smiled brightly and left.

As soon as she'd gone Maisie grabbed my arm. Her fingers were almost as powerful as when she was a mummy.

'You are going to get rid of those gloves and I'm going to watch you.'

I wrenched myself free. 'All right, don't get your knickers in a twist.'

Maisie shoved me back into the bathroom. 'You haven't got long to get ready. Start scrubbing and try to dress less like a tramp. When the party starts, stay in the background and shut up till we get a chance to burn those gloves. Understand?'

I nodded.

She slammed the door shut.

I was trapped.

Chapter Eight
THE PARTY

I thought I was going to pass out with boredom at the party. Apart from random adults from Minty's social groups or Adrian's work, the guests were mostly Maisie's holiday friends and their parents. After Minty had explained who I was, the adults ignored me.

None of Maisie's friends even tried to talk to me. A few glanced at me and sniggered behind their hands. I expect Maisie had told them I was the freaky kid who'd got dumped on her family for the summer. The other girls squealed over Maisie's black dress and gold shoes. It was a good job she'd had a spare. The green dress was squashed at the bottom of the laundry basket, all scrumpled and wet.

Quite a few of the girls were wearing lace gloves. Maisie flinched a bit when they did the

huggy thing, though she disguised it with tinkly giggles and her friends didn't notice.

The boys mostly stood around trying to look cool. All of them fiddled with their mobiles, hoping to get a signal even though they knew it was dodgy in Golden Bay.

I passed the time in a corner, behind two ferns, making up endings to *The Curse of the Hunter's Moon*, mostly involving werewolves breaking into the marquee and eating the guests – messily.

I finally managed to escape when it got dark and the dancing started. Adrian dimmed the main lights; the fairy lights twinkled in the marquee and the flares blazed out in the garden. While the guests 'oohed' and 'aahed' I eased out into the night.

The garden was spectacular, full of fire licking at the darkness and casting bunches of shifting shadows. I leapt in front of the flares burning around the maze and sent a pulled-out shadow looming up the hedge walls. It looked horribly like the liftman. I started making up a rhyme about him gate-crashing the party and sending the guests stampeding out of the marquee like hysterical wildebeest on the Serengeti. What was I thinking? Rhyming was dangerous. I stopped fooling around and went to the Vermin Shed. Better to burn the gloves at once rather than start meddling with magic again.

I stopped by the pond. A breeze wavered the metre high flares burning round it and sent reflections streaming out across the black water. The pond looked like it was catching fire.

'Why aren't you inside?' a familiar voice said.

'I'm getting some fresh air,' I told Minty. I didn't think she needed to know that I was also busy imagining the pool as a lake of fire that the liftman was herding the charging guests into.

Minty frog-marched me back to the marquee. 'It's time for Maisie to open her presents. You should be there.'

She parked me next to Adrian who was inviting his boss to give the first gift to the birthday girl.

'Darling.' She air-kissed Maisie and pressed an oblong present into her hands.

Maisie tore off the expensive wrapping paper and gasped in delight when she saw the leather box inside. It had gold lettering embossed on it, under a silver unicorn. It was the logo of a very, very exclusive designer. Maisie flicked up the clasp, looked inside and screamed.

She hurled the box to the floor and a pair of white lace gloves fell out. Maisie screamed again and then she jumped on them.

'Whatever's the matter?' Minty rescued the gloves and held them out to Maisie.

'No!' Maisie slapped at her mum's hand. 'Get rid of them, they're horrible.'

'Just try them on, Maisie,' Adrian said. I'd never heard him sound angry with her before. She burst into tears and ran out of the marquee and into the house.

'Go after her, Araminta, for goodness sake,' said Adrian. Only he didn't say 'goodness'.

Minty left while Adrian did his best to soothe his boss. It didn't work and she left. The other guests practically fell over themselves in their hurry to follow her. They weren't wildebeest any more – they were rats deserting a sinking ship. I felt sorry for Minty and Adrian.

When everyone had gone, Adrian and I surveyed the deserted marquee and the pile of tastefully arranged presents on the table. It looked like the bridge of the Mary Celeste.

Adrian picked up one of the presents. 'I wonder if we should send them back,' he said.

I shook my head. 'I don't think so. It's not a cancelled wedding and Maisie hasn't been jilted. She's still had an actual birthday. She's entitled to presents.'

I was being practical but it didn't help.

'She made me into a complete fool.'

Minty came back. 'She's distraught.'

'*I'm* distraught,' Adrian said.

Minty's mouth pursed up as though someone had stitched a thread round it and pulled it up tight. It was an expression I'd never seen before. Adrian took one look and headed for the garden mumbling that he was going to douse the flares.

Minty turned her special stare on me.

'What do you know about this?'

'Nothing.' I scrambled after Adrian before Minty could zap me with her death-ray expression. Adrian and I got as far as snuffing out the last of the flares before Minty caught up with us.

'Adrian, you need to talk to Maisie.' She glared and pursed her mouth up again.

He stared back. It was a standoff. I half expected them to whip out weapons and have a full on battle.

Adrian turned to me. 'Finish off here. Remember what I said about safety precautions.'

I nodded, glad to have a chance to avoid the row I saw brewing.

I carted the snuffed out flares to the kitchen garden, double-checked that they were completely dead, and dropped them into the fire pit.

At last I had a chance to get the gloves though I knew burning them wasn't an option now. If Adrian decided to come and check that I'd sorted the flares properly and caught me lighting a fire I'd be in big trouble. And I daren't leave the bag in the shed in case Adrian or the gardener found it by accident. I had to get it back and bring it into the house where I could keep an eye on it.

It was dark inside the shed. I groped my way to the shelf with the jar of nails and fished out the paper bag. There's not much room to hide things in a dress. In the end I stuffed the bag down my back. It made a bulge and was a bit uncomfortable though I was glad to feel the scratchy paper against my skin. I didn't like the thought of a glove touching me. Even the lightest contact might be enough to make me old, or a baby. And what if all three pairs touched me at the same time? Would I keep changing ages or maybe turn into a shrivelled baby?

With thoughts like that I was glad to get back to my bed. It was bad luck that Maisie was sitting on it, waiting. She turned her swollen red eyes on me. 'Have you burnt them?'

The paper crackled faintly against my back. Maisie would have hysterics again if she knew the gloves were close to her.

'No, I still haven't had a chance to get them out of the shed. I'll do it tomorrow, I promise, first thing.'

'I'll get you for this,' Maisie said softly. It was more threatening than the sneers, the jibes and the hysterics.

I grabbed my PJs and fled into the bathroom. By the time I came out again, cautiously, Maisie had gone. I looked for *The Curse of the Hunter's Moon*, and that was gone too. There was no point in looking for it; I was sure Maisie had hidden it, or trashed it just to get back at me. I felt under the bed for one of the stash I kept there. The first one I touched was *PYROMANIAC!* It's not one of my favourites and I hadn't read it in a while. It's about a boy who can start fires just by pointing. It was dull and I fell asleep quickly, dreaming of flames. The flames wavered, orange and yellow and red, filling my eyes with light.

Smoke drifted around me, filled my nose with the smell of burning.

I woke up.

The orange glow and smell of smoke were still there. They were coming from the open window. I leaped out of bed, yanked the window wide and leaned out. Behind the copse at the end of the garden, where the Vermin Shed was, a fire burned madly, flames reaching up to the sky.

Chapter Nine
DISGRACE

The Vermin Shed burned to the ground. I was sorry about it. The gardener had lost all his special gardening tools, Adrian had lost his expensive ones and I'd lost my books. Worse than that though, was that I got the blame.

The fire fighter said the blaze had definitely started with a smouldering flare left against the side of the shed. It had slowly burned its way through the walls and heated the cans of paint inside. Pressure had built up in the tins and eventually the whole lot had exploded with a boom.

As Adrian kept reminding me, I was the one who'd been told to put the flares in the fire pit. He reminded me when the fire brigade had gone, leaving black smoke trickling into the dawn sky. He reminded me over breakfast and again mid-

morning, after he'd tried to contact my mum and dad and failed. He blamed me for that as well. I was grateful to Minty when she said that wasn't my fault.

Adrian grunted and went off to use the landline to try and raise my brothers. There wasn't much chance of that before the afternoon; they work all night and get up at about two in the afternoon. It gave Adrian more time to remind me over lunch that I was an arsonist.

'What I really can't understand,' he said between mouthfuls of broccoli, 'is why you took one flare to the shed when you'd put all the others in the fire pit as I asked you.'

Maisie piped up, 'I bet she wanted to get one of her precious books and used the flare to see inside the shed. Then when she came out, she threw it down without bothering to check if it was properly out.'

It sounded so plausible I couldn't think what to say except, 'I didn't!'

'You must've done,' Maisie said with a self-satisfied smirk. At that moment I knew for sure Maisie was the real culprit. She'd been more scared of the gloves than going into the garden at night and burning the shed down.

'That's enough!' Minty said. I don't know who was more surprised, Maisie or me.

Adrian opened his mouth to protest. Minty did her death-ray stare and he closed it again. We finished the meal in silence.

I knew I was going to be sent home and I didn't want to hang around the house. I decided to go to Franklin's one more time – to get rid of the gloves once and for all.

I fished the bag out from the bottom of the laundry basket where I'd put it, wrapped up in my party dress and sneaked down to the garden. There was a door in the wall enclosing the kitchen garden and using it meant I was less likely to be seen.

Maisie was already there, staring hard at the steaming mound of wet, black ash which was all that was left of the Vermin Shed. She stood well back, as if she was expecting mutant spiders to leap out from the cinders.

'Just checking it's all burned to a crisp, are you?' I said. 'I'm surprised you had the guts to come down here in the dark last night. Why didn't you just bring a torch to look for the gloves?'

She shuddered – a little delicate shudder. 'I wasn't going to risk touching vermin looking for

those... things. It's bad enough in the daylight – spiders and rats...'

'There aren't any rats.'

She laughed. 'Only you.'

'You still didn't need to burn the shed down.'

'I had to make sure they were destroyed.'

'I told you I'd do it.'

'And I should trust you why exactly?'

I didn't bother trying to explain; she'd never believe me.

'Besides,' she said, 'burning down the shed means I get rid of you as well as those... things.'

I didn't care anymore. I'd had enough of Maisie and Minty and Adrian and the whole of Golden Bay. The only thing that bothered me was Mum and Dad having to cut short their magical mystery tour of the east. They'd waited for it for years.

I left Maisie and her smugness and banged through the green door into the cobbled street. I ran down the twisting lanes to Franklin's Emporium. Harriette was going to take the gloves back. My attempts to get rid of them kept going wrong – she could do it instead.

I ran along the promenade and stopped in front of Franklin's. The sun washed over the blue and white frontage, highlighting the seedy, peeling, blue-and-white paintwork. I hesitated. Maybe going in wasn't such a good idea. What if magic started backfiring on me again?

Don't be a wuss, I told myself. The gloves have got to go. Just don't make up any rhymes.

I pushed through the revolving doors and into the marble lobby. It was busy, as usual. I went to the lift where a whole crowd of people waited. The doors slid open, the liftman drew the grille back and we surged in, squashing the old man to one side. He only just had room to press the buttons.

'First floor,' a woman said.

'Second... third... fourth,' called a chorus of voices.

I waited while people poured in and out. It took a while before I was alone with the liftman. I ignored the buzzing and the flashing lights on the call sign, folded my arms and glared. It didn't bother the old man.

'Which floor do you wish?' he asked.

'Whichever one *Harriette's Haberdashery* is on,' I said.

'The Haberdashery is gone.'

Noooo! 'Where?'

The liftman shrugged.

I held up the blue and white striped bag with its three gold crowns. 'What about these gloves?'

'You bought them. They are yours to do with as you please.'

I didn't say what I'd have liked to do with them. 'Basement please,' I said. If Harriette was in Franklin's, I was going to find her.

The lift sank smoothly downwards. The liftman opened the doors and pulled back the grille. 'Basement.'

I moved forward.

'Wait,' the old man said.

I turned.

'Till the next time.'

'There won't be a next time. After this I'm going home and I'm never, ever, coming back here.'

'I'll see you again, soon.' He pulled the grille across and closed the doors. The lift glided upwards.

I covered almost every square centimetre of Franklin's seven floors and unless Harriette was hiding in the Gents she was definitely not there. I was stuck with the gloves.

I ended up in the Terrace Restaurant. The windows were open wide and the room was full

of sunshine, lighting up every corner. It had a new unit serving cream teas. Why not? I thought. I'd earned a cream tea.

I sat down and stared out over Golden Bay and the glittering sea. Boats bobbed in the harbour and donkeys with small children on their backs plodded patiently up and down the beach. It was very peaceful. And boring. If you didn't find yourself accidentally making magic.

The paper bag was on the table and when the waitress came to clear up my empty plate and mug, she reached for it. I snatched it away before she got the chance to touch it.

'Sorry love, thought it was empty,' she said.

I hesitated. What if she did take it? She'd only dump it in the refuse bin. On the other hand, she might look inside, like the gloves and put them on. That wasn't fair to her. The gloves were my responsibility and I had to deal with them.

'It's a present,' I said.

The waitress smiled. 'Lucky thing,' she said and went off to clear another table.

Chapter Ten
GOODBYE, GOLDEN BAY

When I got back to the house Minty and Adrian were waiting for me. They had solemn expressions on their faces. I knew it – I was being sent home in disgrace.

'Your brothers have agreed to take full responsibility for you for the rest of the time your parents are away,' Minty said. 'You're going home first thing tomorrow morning.'

It was hard not to look pleased. I was happy Mum and Dad weren't going to have their second honeymoon interrupted after all and, as a bonus, I was going home to the boys. They were weird but responsible. I'd be OK with them.

A wave of guilt made me rush up and hug Minty.

'I'll miss your cooking,' I said.

I didn't push my luck trying to hug Adrian. He was still convinced I'd burnt down the Vermin Shed.

'I'm sorry about what happened,' I told him. 'I liked working with you in the garden.'

His stony face relaxed a bit. 'I can't say I'm not disappointed, Alex. Apart from this one incident it was a pleasure to have you around.'

A pleasure?

I thought about that while I packed my suitcase. Minty and Adrian had done their best and made me welcome. It was only Maisie who'd made my life difficult. And if it hadn't been for the white lace gloves we'd have settled for avoiding each other.

I didn't see Maisie, apart from at mealtimes, till Minty drove me to the old railway station. Maisie came with us. I suppose she wanted to make sure I'd really gone.

She didn't speak to me until I was safely stowed on the old steam train. I had the whole carriage to myself. There was no corridor, just a door either side with a window you let down with a leather strap.

Minty helped me load my suitcase and bags onto the luggage rack, kissed me goodbye and

got out. I slammed the door shut and lowered the window.

'Thank you for everything, Aunt Minty,' I said. 'And I didn't leave that flare by the shed, truly I didn't.'

Minty looked me straight in the eye. 'We'll never know what really happened.'

Maisie tossed her hair. 'Who else did it then?'

'As I said, we'll never know.'

Maisie flushed.

I was sure Minty suspected Maisie and I was just as sure she'd never admit it even though it wasn't fair. She'd always be on Maisie's side.

The engine coughed, a whistle blew and the train began to shudder as it got up steam. Minty waved. 'Goodbye.'

Maisie pursed up her mouth and made kissy movements with her lips.

'Goodbye, ickle BABY Alex.'

I knew she'd want the last word. I'd come prepared. I whipped out the blue and white striped bag from my pocket. I waved it at her.

She screamed.

I pulled the window shut. The train hauled itself out of the station, picked up speed as it moved round a bend, whistled and surged down the track.

I settled back in the plush, green seat and tucked the bag away. What was I going to do with the gloves? I knew now that magic always comes back on you and I didn't dare throw the gloves away; they'd only reappear. I gave up thinking about them.

As soon as the train was out of Golden Bay my phone pinged. I'd got a proper signal. I rang the boys. Sam promised to be on time picking me up at the station while Ben got lunch. He was waiting on the platform when the train arrived. That was a first. The boys must be taking looking after me seriously.

Sam took my case in one hand and knuckled the top of my head as a welcome home with the other.

'How's the arsonist?' he asked.

'I didn't do it,' I insisted as we set off for the car park.

'Course you didn't,' he said, cheerfully, throwing my suitcase in the boot of his old car.

He and Ben teased me about it all through lunch, which was a pizza and a can of cola. I was already missing Minty's cooking.

'Oh, shut up!' I said in the end. I threw down my crust and started to leave.

'Wait a minute.' Ben pulled me back into my chair. 'Why don't you tell us what really happened.'

I wasn't sure at first. I started to tell them, cautiously, ready to stop if they laughed. They were gripped. They didn't say a word till I'd finished. They looked at each other, then at me.

'You read too much,' Sam said.

That's when they fell about laughing, punching each other on the arms, saying, 'White lace gloves!' and yelling with laughter again.

I gave them my version of Minty's death-stare and stormed out. I was mostly angry because I knew if Ben and Sam didn't believe me, Mum and Dad certainly wouldn't. All I'd be able to do was deny burning down the Vermin Shed without telling them who was really responsible. I was going to have to get rid of the gloves by myself – and I had an idea.

I made my preparations. The first thing I did was get a pair of silver grape-cutter scissors from the cutlery drawer. A friend of Mum's had given them to her one birthday. She never used them and they were all grey and a bit crusty, the way silver goes when it's never polished. I hoped that wouldn't matter; I didn't have time to go hunting for silver polish.

The next thing I did was snap on a pair of rubber gloves for protection against magical contamination. Finally, I went to my room and fetched the paper bag from my wardrobe where I'd stashed the lace gloves.

I went to my desk, emptied the contents of the bag onto it and shivered. It wasn't the draught coming from the open window that made me go cold; it was the gloves. No wonder Maisie had freaked out. All three pairs were exactly what she'd asked for: lacy and fingerless, with a frill round the wrist, but one pair was only big enough to fit a baby's hands, and one was yellowed and stiff with age.

I picked up the scissors and poked the point at the tiny gloves. My plan was to cut them into a squillion pieces and bury the bits in the garden where they'd rot away. I snipped experimentally, which wasn't easy in oversized rubber gloves. A single silky strand came away and entangled itself in the blades. I jiggled the scissors and the entire glove unravelled into one long thread. I hadn't expected that. The second one unravelled in exactly the same way.

I repeated the trick with the brittle old gloves and it worked with them too. And with the third pair. When I'd finished, six strands of lace lay coiled in separate heaps on my desk like dismantled spiders' webs.

I thought furiously. If what I'd read was true, silver could break magic. The problem was, could I do the breaking now I was nowhere near Golden Bay and the liftman? I could only try. A spell came into my head.

I snipped each of the six strands in half and chanted:

'With silver blades your power I sever.
Be gone, O gloves, and come back never.'

A flash of blue and white light, filled with golden sparks, exploded into the air, twisted into a mini vortex and spun out of the window. I watched it dissolve into a faint, glimmering mist until it evaporated into nothing.

That's it, I thought. No more gloves, no more Franklin's Emporium, no more Golden Bay. I leapt around my room, bouncing on the bed like a little kid and yelling in relief.

I should've known better.

EPILOGUE

Mum and Dad believed me when I said I hadn't burned down the shed, and they didn't nag me for an explanation of what had really happened. What they did do was have a long phone conversation with Minty and Adrian. It left them looking thoughtful.

They made quite a few phone calls to Adrian and Minty after that. They also spent a lot of time talking between themselves in soft voices. They stopped when I was around. Even the boys didn't know what was going on.

After a couple of weeks of driving us mad with their whispering Mum and Dad sat us round the table for a family conference. This was going to be big.

Dad plunged straight in. 'You know Adrian's boss was upset by what happened at Maisie's party?'

I had no idea where this was going. 'Yes,' I said cautiously.

'Apparently his relationship with his boss became strained and he applied for a transfer. He's relocating to Manchester.'

'OK.' I had the feeling an axe was going to fall.

'He and Minty want to move as soon as possible and...' Dad took Mum's hand and squeezed it. She nodded.

The axe fell. 'We're buying their holiday house. We're moving to Golden Bay.'

'You're kidding!' This was the worst thing ever.

'How can you afford it?' Ben asked.

'The redundancy payment plus the profit on selling this old house.'

Dad grinned at me. 'Also, because Adrian wanted to sell as soon as possible we got their house at a knock-down price.'

Mum went all dreamy. 'It'll be wonderful. While Dad and I were away we talked about living in a more simple way. I want to set up my own cake-making business and Dad wants to expand his woodworking from a hobby to a job. We can do both those things in Golden Bay. It'll be lovely to start a whole new life.'

I could think of a lot of objections to that but Ben and Sam got in first.

'Not to be selfish or anything...' Ben said.

'... what about us?' Sam finished.

Mum patted Sam's hand. 'You can't afford a studio in London yet but you can have the whole top floor in the new house while you're making your reputations as artists. It's a converted attic with skylights all across the roof. It'll be perfect for a studio.'

'It's all settled then,' I said bitterly.

They were too busy talking and getting excited to hear me. I might as well have been invisible. I went out, the liftman's last words buzzing in my head.

'I'll see you again – soon.'

BONUS BITS!

Test your knowledge of
FRANKLIN'S EMPORIUM

Turn to the back for the answers (no peeking along the way!)

1. Who had bought the present that Maisie threw on the floor?
    a) Uncle Adrian's boss
    b) Uncle Adrian's wife
    c) Uncle Adrian's sister
    d) Uncle Adrian's brother

2. What job do Alex's twin brothers do?
    a) plumbers
    b) artists
    c) shopkeepers
    d) fishermen

3. Where did Alex enjoy visiting most in the old town?
   a) the caves
   b) the rickety old pier
   c) the rockpools on the beach
   d) Franklin's Emporium

4. Where did Alex most like to read?
   a) her bedroom
   b) the Vermin Shed
   c) the garden
   d) the beach

5. What do Maisie and her friends call tourists?
   a) Cockles
   b) Grockles
   c) Sheckles
   d) Winkles

6. On which floor was *Harriette's Haberdashery* the first time Alex went there?
   a) Top floor
   b) Third floor
   c) Basement
   d) Ground floor

7. How much did Alex pay for the second pair of gloves?
   a) £10
   b) £5
   c) £15
   d) £30

8. What was written on the jar label where Alex hid the three pairs of gloves?
   a) nails – large
   b) nails – small
   c) screws – assorted
   d) screws – small

9. What made Maisie scream as Alex left Golden Bay?
   a) Alex pulled a face
   b) The number on the train
   c) Alex stamped on her toe
   d) The blue and white bag

Interesting and Curious words

When reading, do you sometimes think: *'what does that mean?'* or *'why has the author used that word?'* If so, then you are being a good reader as you are thinking about the words! Here are some interesting words used in this book.

redundancy – no longer in employment

'Dad had lost his job and got a big **redundancy** payment.'

reminiscing – enjoying remembering the past

'Mum put the phone away and started **reminiscing**.'

Regency – style of the late 18th and early 19th centuries

'It was a **Regency** house at one end of the sea front.'

mortified – very embarrassed or ashamed

'I know you don't want to come to my party and that's OK because I don't want you there either but Mummy would be **mortified**.'

epaulettes – ornamental shoulder piece on a coat, jacket or military uniform

'And he had **epaulettes**, with gold edging, on his shoulders.'

Mannequins – a dummy used to display clothes in shops

'I had to go down the alleyway of lurching pink **mannequins** to reach it.'

humble – showing a modest feeling about one's own importance

'It came out sort of desperate, although I was trying to sound **humble**.'

wheedle – use flattery to persuade someone to do something or give you something

'Maisie began to **wheedle**.'

manacle – one of two metal bands joined by a chain to fasten a prisoner's hands or feet together, a bit like handcuffs

'The claw squeezed tighter, like a **manacle**.'

daunting – difficult or intimidating to deal with

'I know this kind of grand party might seem **daunting** if you're not used to it but you'll love it if you give yourself a chance.'

WHAT NEXT?

If you enjoyed this book, why not try writing your own story about a magical object or magical shop? Let your imagination run wild but if you're a bit stuck, here are some starting points:

– an item of clothing that allows the wearer to have a type of superpower…

– a shop that changes what it sells based on what the shopper needs…

ANSWERS TO QUIZ

1. a) Uncle Adrian's boss
2. b) artists
3. d) Franklin's Emporium
4. b) the Vermin Shed
5. b) Grockles
6. c) Basement
7. a) £10
8. a) nails – large
9. d) the blue and white bag

COMING SOON!

FRANKLIN'S
EMPORIUM
The Invisicat

Chapter One
BACK TO FRANKLIN'S EMPORIUM

'I'll see you again, soon.'

The voice echoed in my head as I waited for the lift in Franklin's Emporium.

When the old liftman had said those words to me eight months ago I'd almost laughed. I knew there was no way – ever – I was going to come back to the seaside town of Golden Bay and its huge, run-down old department store, Franklin's Emporium. Yet here I was, with my mum, waiting to get into the lift.

The lift pinged and the doors slid open. The liftman pulled aside the black metal grille and Mum went in, trying and failing to see over the pile of *Fran's Fancies* cake boxes in her arms. I stuck as close as possible to her and stared at the floor. I did not want to make eye contact with the liftman.

Mum nudged me with an elbow. 'Move over, there's plenty of room.'

I shuffled grudgingly away, about five centimetres.

'Top floor, Terrace Restaurant, please,' Mum said in her chirpy way.

The lift glided upwards. I sneaked a glance at the liftman. He didn't look any different from how I remembered him. He still wore a smart blue uniform with gold epaulettes and a pocket embroidered with three gold crowns. He stood, tall and gaunt, in his corner, bright eyes peering at me from under huge eyebrows like a hedge in need of trimming. I thought he might say, 'Nice to see you again,' but he didn't speak a word until we got to the top floor.

'Terrace restaurant,' he announced and opened the doors on the busy restaurant.

I nipped in front of Mum. 'I'll guide you.' I steered her out.

'Thank you,' she called over her shoulder to the liftman.

'You're welcome, Madam,' he said in his cracked old voice. The doors shut and the lift

glided downwards.

'Strange old man,' Mum said.

'Too right,' I muttered, leading Mum through the tables to the counter at the far end where a jolly, fattish man was sifting through papers.

He beamed with a grin like a half-moon when he saw us. 'Ah, the cakes – the wonderful cakes!' He trundled out from behind the counter.

'To the kitchen with these.' He took the boxes from Mum and whisked away, backwards, through a pair of swing doors. 'Come!' he bellowed.

Mum shook her head in amused exasperation. 'You don't need to stay. Charles wants to sort out orders for tomorrow and it'll take a while. He's very particular about my cakes.'

She rummaged in her purse for some money. 'Get some treats for Cesare.'

Cesare is her new kitten and she's besotted with it.

'Get a toy for him as well. There's plenty to choose from in the pet shop unit.'

When Franklin's Emporium closed long ago, it became neglected and run down. Then it was sold, re-opened and let out in units. There were all kinds: cafes and coffee shops, second hand

book shops, furniture and toy shops. There was once a haberdashery though that disappeared last summer. The pet shop unit, *Paws 4 Thought*, was on the ground floor but there was no way I was going to take the lift. I walked down all seven flights of stairs so as to avoid the liftman. He was a kind of wizard and I wasn't going to risk getting involved in his magic, not after what happened last summer.

I came out in the grand, marble-floored lobby supported by pillars sculpted with nymphs and fauns. Right in the middle of the vast space was a huge cube of red fabric. It was covering scaffolding that stuck out at the top. As I passed it I heard my brother Ben's voice and a lot of hammering and banging. My brothers were artists and this was one of their installations. I grinned. The inhabitants of Golden Bay were going to get a surprise when the covers came off.

The pet shop unit was tucked away in a corner, on the other side of the lobby. A lot of the units and pop-up shops arrived overnight like mushrooms and disappeared just as suddenly. *Paws 4 Thought* had appeared like that, materialising the day before Cesare sauntered up our garden path and turned my mum's brain to mush.

Mum had picked the kitten up and done the cooing thing. I knew it had cast a spell on her when she instantly forgot about her new bakery project and went hunting for food to stop the kitten's tragic mewing. Up till then Mum had been totally obsessed with setting up her cake and bakery business, *Fran's Fancies*. That was one of the reasons we'd come to live in Golden Bay.

She was going to call the kitten Misty but Dad called him Cesare after some evil old Italian duke, and it stuck – for good reason. Cesare was a complete tyrant: he tore the curtains, scratched the furniture, weed on the carpets and even chewed up my school project. Mum had to write a letter to my teacher saying the cat ate my homework.

For a creature that was adorable – all round blue eyes and smoky grey fur – he had an evil heart. It was the cutesy-pie kitten's fault that the invisicat came to stay and refused to budge.

Paws 4 Thought was bigger than it looked from the outside. The main part was stacked with sacks of cat litter and dog biscuits, birdseed and racks of collars, poop-scoops and bird feeders. The rest was divided into four separate areas: one for fish, one for rodents, one for birds and a private, curtained off area at the back.

The pet shop owner was poking around as if he was trying to find something. When he saw me he flapped his hand irritably, said, 'I'll be with you in a minute,' and started pulling boxes off a shelf and peering behind them.

I didn't mind. It was the Easter holidays and I had time to waste.

Like some other units in Franklin's, *Paws 4 Thought* was strange. It was gloomy, lit by dismal, dusty bulbs. The only bright illumination came from occasional flashes of coloured light from around the edges of the sagging black drapes at the back of the shop.

The pets had fresh food and water but their roomy cages were made of curly, wrought iron metal with bolts and cogs and elaborate locks on the doors. If they'd had wheels they'd have rolled about on their own as if a mad scientist had wound them up. Inside their ornate cages the animals and birds were creepily silent.

In the shadowy aquarium, fish sailed monotonously back and forth in illuminated tanks, occasionally diving down to ruined gothic castles, sunken airships and skulls with jaws that opened and shut. I liked those. I picked up a display skull and was feeding it a simpering mermaid when a jingling noise made me turn.

It was the pet shop owner. He was short and thin with an ordinary face except for the fact it was very, very pale and he had huge ears. An earring, shaped like a snake eating its own tail, hung from the left lobe. He wore a sort of saggy dressing gown in balding black velvet. He was clutching a blue cat collar with three large bells on it. That's where the jingling noise came from.

'Have you lost a cat?' I asked, putting the mermaid back on the shelf.

'None of your business,' he snapped through a mean little mouth. 'What do you want?'

'I'm looking for cat toys,' I said.

'You won't find any in here. Try over there.'

He pointed to a rack near the counter. His finger was encircled by a large ring embossed with another snake.

I went over and browsed. I chose a treat dispenser shaped like a mouse's head. It had a giant pink nose and ears, and holes in the sides for biscuits to fall out of when the cat batted it around. Cesare would like that – he was keen on battering things. I picked up a box of meaty snacks as well.

Two customers came in and I went back to the fish room while the owner was serving them. I thought about feeding the mermaid to a plastic shark. Maybe set up a tug-of-war with the skull?

Maybe not. I didn't want to get a bad reputation, not now Mum and Dad had units here and it was only a couple of days to the boys' exhibition.

I bent down and looked at a blue and gold Siamese fighting fish drifting aimlessly round and round its tank. Staring at me from the other side of the tank was a pair of slanted yellow eyes. I nearly leapt out of my skin.

The eyes vanished.

Strange.

As I leaned forward for a closer look I dropped the box of treats. It rattled. Instantly the eyes appeared again. I picked up the box and shook it experimentally. The eyes moved around the side of the tank to the front, stopped and looked right at me.

When I say, 'the eyes moved,' that's exactly what happened. The eyes. No body, only the eyes. And a loud throbbing purr.